A Note to Parents and Teachers

The *Dorling Kindersley Readers* serie
children which is highly respected
around the world. The LEGO Con
reputation for offering high-quality
specially designed to stimulate a ch
development through play.

Now Dorling Kindersley has joined forces with The LEGO
Company to produce the first-ever graded reading program to
be based around LEGO play themes. Each *Dorling Kindersley
Reader* is guaranteed to capture a child's imagination, while
developing his or her reading skills, general knowledge, and
love of reading.

The books are written and designed in conjunction with
literacy experts, including Dr. Linda Gambrell, President of
the National Reading Conference and past board member of
the International Reading Association.

The four levels of *Dorling Kindersley Readers* are aimed at
different reading abilities, enabling you to choose the books
that are right for each child.

Level 1 – for Preschool to Grade 1
Level 2 – for Grades 1 to 3
Level 3 – for Grades 2 and 3
Level 4 – for Grades 2 to 4

The "normal" age at which a
child begins to read can be
from three to eight years old,
so these levels are only guidelines.

Dorling Kindersley

LONDON, NEW YORK, DELHI,
JOHANNESBURG, MUNICH, PARIS, and SYDNEY

Senior Editor Cynthia O'Neill
Senior Art Editor Nick Avery
Senior Managing Editor Karen Dolan
Managing Art Editor Cathy Tincknell
DTP Designer Jill Bunyan
Production Chris Avgherinos
US Editor Eileen Ramchandran
Reading Consultant Linda B. Gambrell, Ph.D

First American Edition, 2000
2 4 6 8 10 9 7 5 3
Published in the United States by Dorling Kindersley Publishing, Inc.
95 Madison Avenue, New York, New York 10016

Library of Congress Cataloging-in-Publication Data
Birkinshaw, Marie.
Race for Survival / by Marie Birkinshaw.-- 1st American ed.
p.cm. -- (Dorling Kindersley readers)
Summary: The other Rock Raiders try to rescue Axle, who is trapped beneath
a sleeping volcano.
ISBN 0-7894-5458-0 (pbk.) ISBN 0-7894-6096-3 (hc.)
[1. Volcanoes--Fiction.] I. Title. II. Series.

PZ7.B5225 Rac 2000
[Fic]--dc21
99-053293

Color reproduction by Dot Gradations, UK
Printed and bound by L Rex, China

The publisher would like to thank the following for their
kind permission to reproduce their photographs:
c=center; b=bottom; l=left; r=right; t=top

Bruce Coleman Ltd: 10bl; Hans Reinhard 34tl;
Mary Evans Picture Library: 37tr; Le Figaro Magazine:
Philippe Bourseiller 24tl; Robert Harding Picture Library: 18tl, 26tl;
Vulcan 36tl, 47b; © Michael Holford: 38tl; Image Bank: 20clb;
Planet Earth Pictures: 14tk; Science Photo Library: 25tr, 46cl;
Martin Bond 32bl; Matthew Shipp 13tr; NASA 10tl,
39tr,Tainturier/Jerrican 12tl; US Geological Survey/NASA 30tl;
Telegraph Colour Library: 45tr; Vallee 28cla, 28cl; VCL 44tl;
Topham Picturepoint: 22tl, 40tl.

For our complete
catalog visit
www.dk.com

Contents

DORLING KINDERSLEY *READERS*

Race for
SURVIVAL

Written by Marie Birkinshaw • Illustrated by Roger Harris

Level
4
GRADES 2-4

A Dorling Kindersley Book

The story so far...

The LEGO Rock Raiders are an intrepid team of scientists, engineers, and miners. They explore deep space in search of valuable minerals and crystals to bring back home.

Chief
Captain of the
LMS Explorer

Six months ago, their spaceship, the *LMS Explorer*, was hit by an asteroid and badly damaged. The Rock Raiders were trapped in the orbit of an uncharted planet.

Docs
Commander
and geologist

Luckily, Planet U contained rich sources of LEGO ore, as well as power crystals – the purest form of fuel in the galaxy. The Rock Raiders descended beneath the planet's surface. They were able to excavate LEGO ore and power crystals, to energize the ship's engines and travel home.

Jet
Flight
Lieutenant
and pilot

Now the Rock Raiders have traveled back to Planet U – this time, on a fact-finding mission.

Planet U is a mysterious world, on the far side of the galaxy. Its structure is completely unlike our own planet. Volcanic areas sit side-by-side with limestone caves, icy underground lakes, and marble caves, studded with gemstones.

Massive creatures, called Rock Monsters, live in the underground tunnels and feed on power crystals.

Now read on....

Axle
Midshipman
and driver

Sparks
Midshipman
and engineer

Bandit
Sub-Lieutenant
and helmsman

Trapped!

Axle switched off the engine of the LEGO Chrome Crusher. He wiped his hand over his forehead.

"Mining is such hot work," the Rock Raider grumbled. "It's a shame there's no chance of a cool breeze two miles underground."

Axle pushed a button on the Chrome Crusher. The engine started up again and the steel drill began to cut through the solid rock.

Axle peered at the massive walls. He was hoping to spot a vein of LEGO ore in the stone.

This was a routine mission. Axle was checking levels of LEGO ore in Quadrant 14, one of the unexplored regions of Planet U.

If he found some ore, he could hurry back to headquarters for a well-earned rest.

Mining
Digging and excavating underground, to find useful stones and metals, has been carried out for thousands of years. Coal, gold, and silver are all mined from the Earth.

Ore
Most useful metals are mixed within other rocks. This source is called the ore. Metals need to be extracted from the ore after mining.

Hematite,
iron ore

Methane

Methane is also known as natural gas, and is found in underground rocks. It is a danger for miners because it is flammable and may cause explosions when it mixes with air.

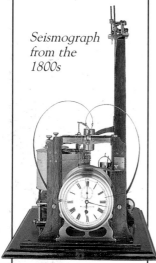

Seismograph from the 1800s

When the Earth shakes

Scientists record the strength of a ground tremor using an instrument called a seismograph.

From time to time, Axle checked the instruments panel on the Chrome Crusher. He needed to keep an eye on the working conditions underground, especially since he was alone today. Scanners were built into the Chrome Crusher, to warn him of any potential risks.

"Methane levels okay? – Check," muttered Axle. He flicked a small switch. It showed that there was no build-up of poisonous, explosive gases in the tunnel.

Conditions in the mine seemed stable. Axle had no warning that disaster was about to strike.

He was just too hot.

Then, suddenly, the walls of the tunnel seemed to tremble. The drill made a bucking movement and lurched forward.

Axle lost his balance. He almost fell beneath the wheels as the Chrome Crusher tilted onto its side.

At the same time, he heard a roar in the rocks above him. Boulders began to crash from the roof of the tunnel and break into razor-sharp splinters.

"Ground tremor!" Axle thought, trying not to panic. "It's time to get out of here!"

But he was already too late.

Drills
Rock drills are often hollow. Water is pumped down the middle, to help carry away waste materials and keep the drill bit cool.

Asteroid
These are irregular-sized rocks, in orbit through space. Many are over 60 miles across.

Planet exploration
Humans have not visited any other planets yet. However, thanks to data sent back by space probes, we know a little about nearby worlds.

The Voyager *space probe*

To the rescue

On the *LMS Explorer*, Sparks had just taken over the radio controls. It was a quiet shift. Everything seemed to be running smoothly on Planet U.

Sparks smiled to himself as he remembered the Rock Raiders' first mission to the planet.

After the huge asteroid hit the *Explorer*, the team had faced a risky mission to the planet surface. They had come across Rock Monsters, Ice Monsters, and burning lakes of lava as they searched for power crystals.

Luckily, the search had all been worth it in the end.

Now the Rock Raiders were back. They had come to analyze the rocks on Planet U in detail.

As Sparks thought back over the earlier trip, Axle's voice crackled over the radio.

"Mayday! Mayday! Can anyone hear me? Axle to headquarters!"

His voice was very faint.

"What's wrong, Axle?" called Sparks, grabbing the radio.

"I'm in trouble, dude!" Axle replied. "There's been a tremor in Quadrant 14 and now I'm trapped in a tunnel. My oxygen purifier won't work for much longer..., I need help soon, guys...."

Then the radio faded out.

Mayday
The distress signal "Mayday" is recognized around the world. It first came from a French phrase *"M'aider!"* – which means "Help me!"

Tremors
A tremor is a minor earthquake, caused by movements in the crust, or surface, of the Earth. Most earthquakes are too faint to be felt, but some cause terrible devastation.

Geology
The modern science of geology was founded by James Hutton in the 18th century. It is the study of how the Earth changes, how it was formed and what rocks are made of.

Engineer
An engineer is trained to build or design complicated machinery or structures — from cars to skyscrapers!

The *Explorer's* rescue vehicles were always ready for an emergency. The vehicles carried drilling and digging tools. There were medical supplies, too, in case a Rock Raider was injured.

As soon as Chief heard about Axle, he handpicked a rescue crew.

Docs led the team. He was a brilliant scientist who had studied geology for years. He would decide if the rockfall was a warning that a bigger tremor was on the way.

Jet, the pilot, was known across the galaxy for her flying skills. Sparks was the best engineer in space. He could mend almost any machine. And Bandit, the *Explorer's* gruff navigator, was fearless and quick-thinking in a crisis.

"We only have approximate coordinates for Axle's location, based on his log from yesterday," Chief said.

"You're in a race against time – find Axle before he uses up his available air.

"This is a dangerous mission," Chief added. "That quadrant was once a volcanic area. Our scanner readings show that all of the volcanoes are dormant now.

"But *something* caused that tremor – so be careful down there."

Volcano
We often think of a volcano as a cone-shaped mountain.
In fact, a volcano is any hole through which molten rock (magma) from inside a planet reaches its surface.

Dormant
Between eruptions, a volcano is said to be dormant. Sometimes, volcanoes are dormant for hundreds of years between eruptions.
An extinct volcano is one that will never erupt again.

Quadrant 14

The Rock Raiders reached Quadrant 14 in half an hour. It was a hostile place, where geysers spat boiling water into the air.

The team had traveled to a small mountain. Basalt crunched under their feet as they looked up at tunnel entrances. The tunnels had been carved out by Rock Monsters over hundreds of years.

Geysers
Geysers are underground springs that shoot out steam and hot water.

"Axle was exploring that tunnel on the left of the mountain," Docs told them. "Sparks, take a Granite Grinder down there. Jet, you follow him on a Hover Scout."

"I'll take the Rapid Rider," said Bandit. "Perhaps there's a rescue route via the underground rivers."

Docs grabbed a Hover Scout.

"I'm going to investigate that tremor," he said.

Basalt

Volcanic rocks Many rocks were formed by volcanic action, when magma from the core of the Earth cooled and hardened on the surface. Basalt is a volcanic rock.

Granite
All rocks
are made of
different kinds
of chemicals,
called minerals.
Granite is made
of quartz, mica,
and feldspar.
It is either
pink or gray,
depending on
the kind of
feldspar it
contains.

Sparks and Jet drove quickly through the winding tunnels.

Two miles below ground, boulders blocked the track.

"This is the place," said Sparks, stopping the Granite Grinder. "Axle grumbled yesterday that he'd only found granite in Quadrant 14."

"Listen, Sparks," said Jet, looking relieved. "He's sending us a signal!"

Sparks listened closely.

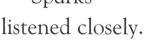

Morse Code
This form of communication was developed by a US inventor named Samuel Morse (1791–1872). In the code, short or long beeps represent letters of the alphabet.

He could hear a faint tapping. Jet was right. On the other side of the rockfall, Axle was using old-fashioned Morse code to signal to his rescuers. The rocky walls were carrying the sound. "He heard the Grinder's engine," Jet said. "He tapped 'What took you so long?'"

Jet used a chisel to tap back, 'We're on our way!'

Chisels
The tools that rock collectors need to gather rock samples include square-head hammers and a range of chisels.

17

Underground waterways
There is much more water below the Earth than above it. Rain water seeps under the ground and fills the underlying rockbed with water, which collects in pools and streams.

Oxygen
We cannot see, taste, or smell oxygen, but it makes up 20% of the Earth's atmosphere and we cannot live without it!

But Sparks seemed worried. He pointed to his scanner.

"We need to change our plan," he told Jet. "The first tremor damaged the roof of this tunnel. If we drill through to Axle, we could bring the whole thing down."

"Let's radio the others!" Jet said.

"No, they should keep searching," Sparks replied. "Bandit could find a waterway on the other side of those rocks, and reach Axle quickly.

"And Docs must find out what caused the tremor in the first place."

Sparks paused and bit his lip. He was thinking hard.

"We could dig Axle out, but there's no time to send back to HQ for the Loader Dozer. Axle's oxygen purifier will stop working in about 30 minutes. He'll run out of air."

Sparks frowned at Jet.

"It looks like we're going to get our hands dirty," he said.

Simple machines
Not all machines are big and noisy. Some are small, and carry out simple jobs – ramps, levers, and wheels are all examples. Whatever its size, a machine makes a job easier to do.

Levers
Levers make it easier to move heavy objects. They come in many different forms – for example, a wheelbarrow is a kind of lever.

There was a LEGO beam in the back of the Granite Grinder. Sparks dragged it over to the pile of rocks and put one end beneath a boulder.

"This will lever the rocks out of the way," he told Jet. "It's a simple machine and we need all the help we can get."

But after ten minutes, they had only shifted a small pile of boulders.

And worse, there had been no other Morse signals from Axle.

"He's never *this* quiet," said Jet. "Not even with a hundred tons of rock on top of him. We have to contact the others, Sparks."

Sparks didn't reply. Jet glanced back to check that he was okay – and gave a gasp of horror.

A Rock Monster was standing behind them, with its mighty arms held up high. It held a massive rock in its hands, ready to crash down on their heads.

Trouble!

Jet and Sparks stared at the Rock Monster. Behind them there was only a blocked tunnel. There was no way they could escape.

The monster dropped the rock to one side. It lunged toward them. Sparks closed his eyes.

The monster pushed past the Rock Raiders and bent down to the boulders that blocked the tunnel.

Monster myths
Huge footprints, seen in the snow on the Himalayas, are said to belong to a monster called the yeti.

With incredible power, it plucked the rocks up and flung them aside, as if they were cardboard.

In ten minutes, the monster had cleared a way through the stones. It immediately squeezed into the gap. The Rock Raiders could hear it pushing boulders out of the way, as it carried on through the tunnel.

"Will it hurt Axle?" said Sparks.

"It didn't hurt us," said Jet.

The Rock Raiders pushed through the gap to find their friend.

"Axle, are you okay?" called Jet.

There was no answer.

Sharp splinters of serpentine and obsidian littered the floor of the tunnel. The massive Chrome Crusher was still lying on its side. The Rock Raiders guessed that Axle had sheltered beneath it, to escape the falling rocks.

But Axle – and the Rock Monster – had disappeared.

Serpentine
This rock contains streaks of green and red, just like a serpent's skin, which explains its name!

Obsidian
This shiny, black rock looks like polished glass. It has sharp edges, and so early people often used it to make tools and weapons.

Magma
The molten rock inside the Earth is called magma. When it erupts on the surface, it is known as lava.

Taking the temperature
Lava is very hot – about 2,000°F. When scientists want to collect lava samples, they stand at a safe distance and use a long metal rod to hook up a molten blob!

Docs in danger

Docs was exploring the tunnels in nearby Quadrant 15 when the second tremor started.

It began with a low rumble. The rocks seemed to be roaring with anger. Slivers of granite started to fall from the rocky ceiling.

Then the floor cracked open. Boiling magma from the planet's core erupted through the split rock.

All at once, it was incredibly hot. Docs turned his Hover Scout and fled through the tunnels. He swooped and swerved, taking short cuts wherever he could.

Behind him, the melted rock swallowed everything in its path.

It took all of Docs' strength and concentration to outpace the magma flow. Just when he thought he could no longer go on, he saw a gap in the walls high above him.

With a final spurt of strength, Docs pointed the Hover Scout up and flew through the gap to safety.

Eruptions
Some volcanoes shoot out lava, ash, rock, and gas. Others erupt quietly – lava just flows down the sides of the volcano.

The Ice Monster

Potholes
Underground caves or riverbeds are known as potholes. Some people, known as spelunkers, explore these caves using specialized equipment.

Bandit steered the Rapid Rider along a narrow underground stream. He was looking for a new route through to Axle.

It was very cold on the water. Bandit pulled on some gloves.

"Five more minutes," he muttered. "Then I'll go back."

Fifty yards on, the air was so cold that it hurt to breathe.

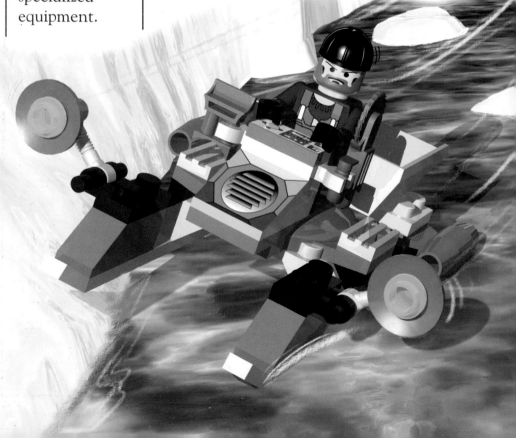

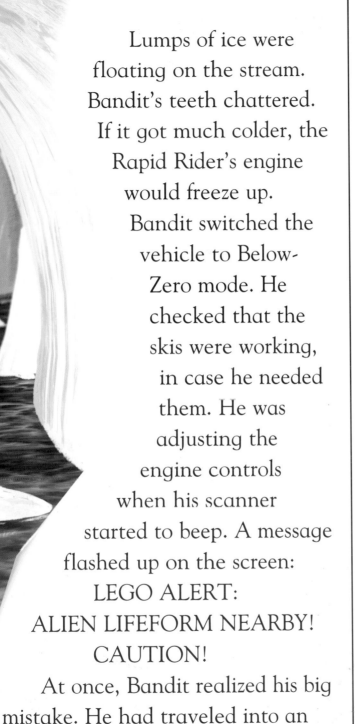

Lumps of ice were floating on the stream. Bandit's teeth chattered. If it got much colder, the Rapid Rider's engine would freeze up.

Bandit switched the vehicle to Below-Zero mode. He checked that the skis were working, in case he needed them. He was adjusting the engine controls when his scanner started to beep. A message flashed up on the screen:
LEGO ALERT:
ALIEN LIFEFORM NEARBY!
CAUTION!

At once, Bandit realized his big mistake. He had traveled into an Ice Monster's den.

Ice
Water becomes solid when the temperature drops below 0°C (32°F). As it freezes, it becomes less dense than in its liquid state. This is why ice floats on water.

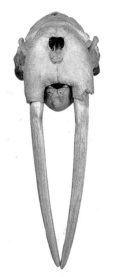

Walrus tusks

Frozen wastes
Polar animals adapt to the cold conditions. Most have an extra layer of fat to keep warm, while the walrus climbs ice with its tusks!

Cave dwellers
Many cave-dwelling animals, such as bats, have adapted so well to their dark homes that they have very poor eyesight.

Lighting the dark
The first safety lamps were developed in the 1700s. They helped miners see in the dark mines, where there was often explosive gas, without using a naked candle flame.

The monster had sensed him. As Bandit looked around, it reared out of the water, roaring with fury, its glacial claws sharp as steel.

Bandit didn't have time to reach for his Freezer beam. The Ice Monster had already caught hold of the Rapid Rider. Grasping the side of the boat, it gave a mighty shove and smashed the vehicle against the cavern wall.

The Ice Monster slipped back under the freezing stream.

Bandit was sore all over, but not badly hurt. And although the main light on the Rapid Rider was slightly damaged, it still gave out a faint glow.

But the skis were a problem. One
of them was too damaged to repair.
When he discovered that his radio
was broken as well, Bandit knew it
was time for some quick thinking.

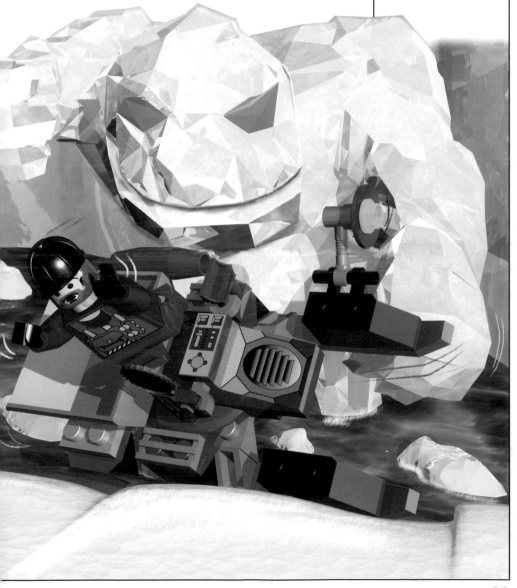

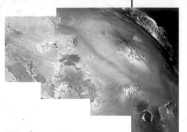

Warning sign

The second tremor was a terrible warning. Docs flew to catch up with Jet and Sparks.

"This mountain is an active volcano," he cried, jumping off the Hover Scout. "That's what caused the ground tremors. The pressure is building – this place is going to blow in two hours. We've got to hurry."

"But we've lost Axle!" said Jet.

"We think he went this way," added Sparks, pointing to a gaping hole, half-hidden behind a crag of rock. A passage behind it led down toward darkness.

"Let's follow him," said Docs.

Leaving the vehicles behind, the Rock Raiders walked into the dark.

The passage led to a massive cave, carved out of the marble. The roof was as high as a skyscraper.

"Wow!" gasped Jet. "This is like a fairytale cavern!"

Stalagmites towered around them, tall as church spires. Gems glittered against the walls.

In the middle of the cave was a dark blue lake. And glowing LEGO power crystals were piled around the water's edge.

Gemstones
A gemstone is a mineral that is valued for its great beauty or rarity.

Quarry
A quarry is an area cut out of the ground so that minerals or stone can be dug from the surface.

On the other side of the cavern, a Rock Monster was fast asleep. It looked as if it were supposed to be on guard duty. A few yards from the monster, Axle was kneeling by a cluster of crystals.

"Good to see you," said Docs.

"I'm glad you found your way down here," Axle smiled back.

"What is this place?" Sparks whispered in amazement.

"It's a crystal quarry, I think," said Docs, quietly. "A Rock Monster secret. I'm not surprised they guard it. I've never seen so many power crystals."

"There was a hidden entrance in the tunnel. I found it as I searched for an escape route," said Axle.

"So that's why the Rock Monster moved the boulders," said Sparks. "He was hungry."

Behind them, the Rock Monster sentry snored loudly.

"He ate too much," said Axle, with a grin.

"It's an incredible find," said Docs. "I can't wait to lead an expedition back here, with the right equipment. But right now we should head back to the ship. Jet, please radio Bandit and ask him to head back to HQ."

Crystals
Rock crystals are a type of see-through quartz (a mineral). People once thought that crystals were made of ice, frozen so hard that it would not melt!

Expedition
Throughout history, people have set out on journeys, or expeditions, to discover unknown places. Such trips need lots of planning.

Slugs
Slugs belong to a group of mollusks called gastropods, which means "stomach feet." On Earth, garden slugs grow to about one inch, while the great gray slug is a massive six inches long!

As he finished speaking, an angry bellow echoed around the underground lake. It came from a cave on the other side of the deep blue water.

The noise woke the Rock Monster sentry, who jumped up and pounded toward the cave. The Rock Raiders were close behind him.

Inside the cave, three Rock Monsters were defending the quarry against a giant slug. Although the Rock Monsters were strong, the slug was as big as all three of them.

As the slug tried to gobble some crystals, the Rock Monsters sounded an alarm. More Rock Monsters ran in. They pelted the slug with rocks.

The slug was outnumbered.
It squelched back into the shadows,
leaving a thick slimy trail behind it.
"Yuck! Gross!" said Sparks, as
the Rock Monsters picked up their
crystals and left the cave.

Slime
As a slug
crawls along,
it leaves a
slimy trail.
The type of
slime changes
when the slug
is under attack.

35

Race against time

Docs checked his scanner.

"We've seen some amazing things today, but now we really should move," he said. "Pressure is rising all the time and... oh, my!"

Docs looked up.

"We don't have much time. There's going to be a major eruption, very soon," he said.

"How can you tell?" asked Jet.

"There's a kind of magma reservoir beneath this cavern," Docs explained. "It's under pressure and magma levels are building up."

Volcanologists
Scientists who watch, record, and try to understand volcanoes are called volcanologists, after Vulcan, the Roman god of fire.

"So?" asked Axle.

"The tunnel network leading from this cavern is going to act like a feeder pipe," Docs told him. "It's going to carry the magma to the surface."

Docs pointed to the scanner.

"This explosion could blow the side off the mountain," he said. "We need to get well away. *Now.*"

"We can't leave – we have to warn the Rock Monsters," said Jet.

"Yes," agreed Axle. "Those big guys have never done us any harm. They've even helped us out."

"We have to try to make them understand us," Jet added.

"I don't think we can," Docs told her. "It has never worked before."

"But there is a way we can save them," Sparks said. "I think we can contain the spread of the magma so that it doesn't make it to the surface of the mountain."

Biggest bang! In 1883, the volcano on the island of Krakatoa exploded. It made the loudest noise ever recorded and could be heard over 3,000 miles away, in Australia. It caused massive flooding and destruction.

Volcano gods
Early people created myths to explain volcanoes. The Hawaiian goddess Pele was said to live inside a fiery volcano crater! She had the power to make mountains and islands or destroy rocks and forests.

Sparks' idea was simple, but not all the Rock Raiders agreed with it.

"You can't destroy the Chrome Crusher!" said Axle.

"We have to," said Sparks. "We must block the tunnels leading from this cavern. The melted rock from the planet's core won't be able to force its way up and through the mountain. This cavern will survive, and so will the Rock Monsters."

"But why my Chrome Crusher?" argued Axle.

"When the laser blows up, the explosion will be more powerful than if we just used dynamite on its own. The extra blast will ensure that we block the tunnels with rocks," said Sparks.

"Don't worry, Axle," Docs said. "We'll build you a new one."

As Sparks rigged explosives, Jet tried to radio Bandit, with no luck.

Olympus Mons
The largest volcano in our whole family of nearby planets is Olympus Mons, on Mars. It is three times as high as Mount Everest.

Mysterious explosion

In 1908, a massive explosion, as powerful as a nuclear blast, destroyed thousands of miles of a Siberian forest. We now know the blast was caused by the shockwaves when an asteroid burst above Earth's atmosphere.

Explosives

Explosives are unstable. They produce a sudden release of energy and a rapid build-up of gas, leading to a high pressure blast.

Axle checked that no Rock Monsters were lurking in the shadows. Luckily, he could see no sign of them.

Sparks had rigged detonators at key points in the tunnels.

"I've set the timer. Let's move," he told the team.

The Rock Raiders had to be far from the cavern before the explosion. Sparks pushed the Granite Grinder into top gear, while Axle hopped on the back of Jet's Hover Scout. The team began the race to safety.

Five minutes later, they heard a CRUMP! as the bombs went off.

"There she goes," sighed Axle.

"The Rock Monsters won't be able to use their quarry for awhile," said Docs. "But when things cool down, they'll go back."

Jet swerved as a stalactite fell from the roof, blocking the tunnel.

"Keep back!" called Sparks.

He pulverized the stalactite with the Granite Grinder's drill, clearing a route through the passageway.

"Still no contact from Bandit," worried Jet, as the Rock Raiders sped towards the tunnel exit. "I hope he was nowhere near that cavern."

Stalactite
These amazing "icicles of rock" hang from the ceilings of limestone caves. They form as water drips down the rock over the years, each drip leaving behind a tiny deposit of minerals.

The volcano blows

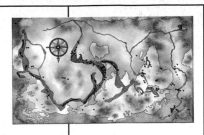

Finally, as the Rock Raiders drew near to the tunnel exit, the underground pressure boiled over.

In the marble cavern, the walls shivered as magma tried to force a way out of the mountain. Gemstones rained from the roof. But after the massive explosion, every tunnel was blocked with rock. Amazingly, the magma did not push through.

"Keep going, everyone," Docs urged. There was still a danger that poisonous gases would be released by the explosion. The team needed to scramble clear of the tunnels.

Where on Earth?
Most of the world's active volcanoes are either on the West Coast of America, or in Japan and East Asia. This area is known as the Ring of Fire.

Poison gas
Volcanologists wear masks for protection against poison gases and choking dust.

Dams
These barriers are usually built across rivers, either to stop flooding or to provide water and electricity to nearby towns and villages.

The makeshift dam had held, and the Rock Monsters were saved. But there was no sign of Bandit on the mountain slopes outside.

"Where is he?" asked Jet. "Can anyone see him?"

Axle gave a loud laugh.

"Look over there!" he said.

Bandit was coming toward them, on a homemade snow board.

"My own invention," he said, as he skated up to them. "An unfriendly Ice Monster wrecked the Rapid Rider. So I made this from a spare ski!

"Now is anyone going to tell me what those loud noises were about?"

"Let's get back to HQ," smiled Docs, as the others crowded around Bandit. "Looks like we all have some tales to tell!"

Snow boarding
Snow boarders use both feet to control their snow board.

Volcano facts

A volcano is a hole in the surface of a planet, through which molten rock, ash, or gas from the inside of the planet reaches the surface.

The surface of the Earth is made of vast slabs of rock, called plates. They are slowly moving apart. Where this happens, molten rock inside the planet is forced upward in a volcanic eruption.

Beneath a volcano is a chamber of red-hot molten rock. This is pushed to the surface by hot gases.

Wherever plates are moving apart, there are tremors (earthquakes), too. There are over a million quakes every year, but most are too small to be felt.

There are about 1,500 volcanoes on land and more beneath the seas.

Most volcanoes lie in an area called the Ring of Fire, around the edge of the Pacific Ocean.

In AD 79, Mount Vesuvius exploded in Italy. It buried the town of Pompeii in hot ash. The ash preserved food, objects, and the shape of people's bodies. The remains tell us about the Roman way of life.

Before the explosion, Vesuvius had been dormant for 800 years!

In 1963, an undersea volcano exploded near Iceland. The explosion formed a new island, called Surtsey.

Volcanologists spend years trying to predict the next volcanic explosion. But even after all their research, we still cannot predict the exact time of an eruption.

Glossary

Basalt
A dark, heavy volcanic rock.

Coordinates
A set of numbers that pinpoint the position of a place or location.

Crust
The rocky outer surface of the Earth.

Crystals
Solid materials that grow in a regular shape, such as a cube or a column. Many minerals come in the form of crystals.

Dormant
When a volcano is dormant, it is "sleeping" and not expected to erupt for awhile.

Geologist
A scientist who specializes in the study of the Earth and its structure.

Lava
Extremely hot, melted rock that has erupted from a volcano to reach the surface of a planet. Lava is so hot that it can melt steel. Also see magma.

Log
Pilots and sailors make detailed records of their journeys in a log, or logbook.

Magma
Magma is melted rock, under the surface of a planet. Also see lava.

Marble
A smooth rock that is formed from another rock, called limestone. When underground limestone is exposed to great heat and pressure over thousands of years, it changes to marble.

Methane
A gas, also known as natural gas. It is produced underground, as dead animal or plants slowly decay.

Mineral
Any naturally occurring substance that is not formed from a plant or animal – for example, a rock or metal.

Navigator
Someone who plans the direction that a vehicle, such as a ship or plane, should take.

Obsidian
A black volcanic rock that looks like glass.

Ore
Any mineral or rock that contains a metal is called an ore. The rocks are mined and processed to extract the metal.

Radar
Radio Detection and Ranging. A way of detecting objects by sending out radio waves and collecting the "echoes."

Serpentine
A red-green rock.

Stalactites
Spikes of rock, growing down from the roof of a limestone cave.

Stalagmites
Pillars of rock that grow upward, from the floor of a limestone cave.

Transmission
The act of sending a message from one place to another, using radio waves or electrical signals.

Tremor
A minor earthquake.

Volcano
The gap or hole in the surface of a planet, where hot, liquid rock reaches the surface.

Volcanologist
A scientist who watches and records volcanic action, to try and predict when a volcano will erupt.